DO NOT TAKE YOUR DRAGON ON A FIELD TRIP

WRITTEN BY JULIE GASSMAN   ILLUSTRATED BY ANDY ELKERTON

CAPSTONE EDITIONS

a capstone imprint

You've been marking the calendar. The day's finally here!
The day you've been waiting for—the best day of the year!

It's time for the field trip, and you're ready to go.
But before you head out, there's one thing you should know . . .

Before you leave school and head to the bus,
your teacher will have some rules to discuss.

He'll assign chaperones who won't be prepared
for a big, scaly student who will leave them quite **scared!**

Once on the bus the real trouble will start.
Your dragon will kick off the trip with a **fart**.

And that spiky tail needs a seat of its own,
leaving little room for a scared chaperone.

When you're on a field trip, you represent your school.
Manners are important, so follow each rule.

But your dragon's rudeness will take its toll,
when she goes on and on with her
stop, drop, and **roll.**

When it's time for a tour, things won't improve.
Your dragon will fall behind as you move.

Once back in line he'll demand you go faster.
He'll touch the wrong thing. It will be a **disaster!**

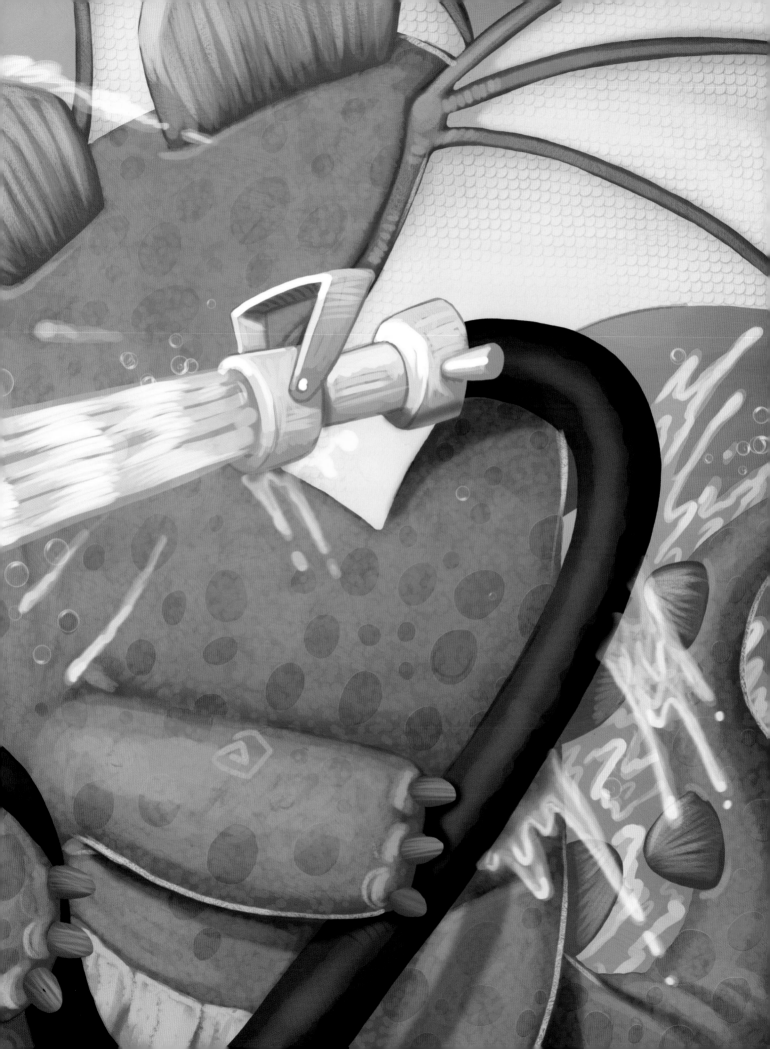

Whipping around, her tail hits your arm.
Next thing you know, **you've** hit an alarm!

She'll use a loud voice. She'll interrupt.
She'll bump into your friends and might even **erupt!**

SO DO **NOT** TAKE YOUR DRAGON ON A FIELD TRIP!

But I've told him about this field trip for weeks.
If I tell him no now, tears will roll down his cheeks.

He deserves an adventure . . . to learn something new!
Please, oh, **please**, can't he go too?

Sometimes we cannot do all we desire,
especially when it puts us at risk of a fire.

But you can still help your dragon learn something new.
Listen to me now, here's what you should do.

Share field trip facts that leave him in awe.
Draw him some pictures of all that you saw.

And as soon as you can, take his wing in your grip . . .

AND TAKE YOUR **DRAGON** ON HIS OWN FIELD TRIP!

ABOUT THE AUTHOR

The youngest in a family of nine children, Julie Gassman grew up in Howard, South Dakota. After college, she traded in small-town life for the world of magazine publishing in New York City. She now lives in southern Minnesota with her husband and their three children. Julie's favorite field trip was visiting the zoo, where she spent lots of time watching the gorillas.

ABOUT THE ILLUSTRATOR

After 14 years as a graphic designer, Andy decided to go back to his illustrative roots as a children's book illustrator. Since 2002 he has produced work for picture books, educational books, advertising, and toy design. Andy has worked for clients all over the world. He currently lives in a small tourist town on the west coast of Scotland with his wife and three children.

Do NOT Take Your Dragon on a Field Trip is published by
Capstone Editions, a Capstone imprint
1710 Roe Crest Drive, North Mankato, Minnesota 56003
capstonepub.com

Copyright © 2019 Capstone Editions

Library of Congress Cataloging-in-Publication Data
Names: Gassman, Julie, author. | Elkerton, Andy, illustrator.
Title: Do not take your dragon on a field trip / written by Julie Gassman; illustrated by Andy Elkerton.
Description: North Mankato, Minnesota: Capstone Editions, [2019] |
Summary: When dragons are banned from accompanying students on a visit to the firestation, for such reasons as rudeness, farting, and a spikey tail, children find the perfect field trip for the scaly creatures.
Identifiers: LCCN 2018060530 | ISBN 9781684460595 (hardcover) | ISBN 9781684468188 (paperback)
Subjects: | CYAC: Stories in rhyme. | Dragons—Fiction. | School fieldtrips—Fiction
Classification: LCC PZ8.3.G199 Di 2019 | DDC [E]—dc23
LC record available at https://lccn.loc.gov/2018060530

Designer: Nathan Gassman

Printed and bound in China. PO5557